KICKBACK KID

Kelly took the snap from center. He held it in his outstretched arms. He dropped the ball. His foot came up to meet it. His toe connected solidly with the falling ball. The ball took off like a shot.

The ball went straight up into the air! It slowly curved backward, heading the wrong way down the field. It dropped to the gridiron and kept rolling toward Santa Clara's goal.

The fumbled punt went 25 yards...

—the wrong way!

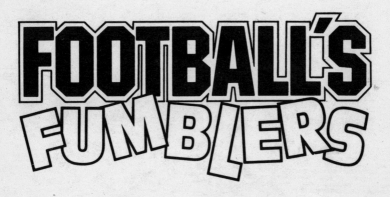

FOOTBALL'S FUMBLERS

Written by D. J. Arneson

Illustrated by Pamiel Barcita

Packaged by Paterson Productions, Inc.

Western Publishing Company, Inc., Racine, Wisconsin 53404

FOOTBALL'S FUMBLERS

Football is a game of precise rules and carefully planned plays. From the coach to the last man in the lineup, everyone knows exactly what to do.

But what happens when the wind blows the wrong way?

What does a player do when his pants fall down?

Where does a runner run after he's run 100 yards to the wrong end zone?

What do you call a kicker who decides to try to pass instead of punt?

When the unexpected happens in football, anything can happen. And it does!

Football's Fumblers contains hilarious examples of the wacky way things go wrong on the gridiron.

THE WATER BOY SNEAK

Georgia Bulldogs vs. Alabama—1912

Today's football players dress like tanks. From battering ram helmets to super-grip running shoes, football teams wear hi-tech armor. It wasn't always that way. One year the Georgia Bulldogs' uniforms included a pair of coveralls like a mechanic— or a water boy— might wear.

It was part of a trick play. The idea was to hide a player. But how do you hide someone on an open field? Easily. The Bulldogs dressed a player in white coveralls. They handed him a water bucket and told him to stand on the sidelines.

It worked. Everyone who saw the white-suited guy with the bucket presumed he was the water boy. But the minute the ball was snapped, the player dropped his bucket *and* his disguise.

When the quarterback stepped back to pass, the "water boy" ran down the field. Nobody realized he was a player until it was too late. The quarterback tossed a pass to the bogus "boy." He ran halfway down the field before Alabama caught on and tackled the runaway "water boy."

PANTYWAIST PUNT

Sean Landeta, New York Giants, 1986

Baseball players get three swings to hit the ball. Football punters get one. In baseball the pitcher throws the ball. All the kicker has to do is drop it. His foot does the rest. That should guarantee a "home run" every time. Not always.

Sean Landeta set himself for the snap. His team, the New York Giants, and their opponents, the Chicago Bears, were tied, 0-0. Landeta was on his own goal line. He had to kick the ball as high and far as he could to drive the Bears away.

The ball zipped into Landeta's hands. He planted one foot firmly on the turf. He cocked his other leg for the punt. He had practiced this a thousand times. A solid kick would send the Bears to midfield. Landeta let the ball fall. He kicked with all his might.

Landeta's kick had enough force to knock the bumper off a car. But it barely touched the ball! The ball wobbled across the 5-yard line.

Shaun Gayle of the Bears saw the fumbled kick. He raced forward. He grabbed the ball and flew across the goal line to score. Sean Landeta's bumbled punt went into the record books. It had traveled seven yards— backward!

11

The original "wrong-way" runner, Roy Riegels, turns a recovered fumble into the most famous wrong-way run in football history.

WRONG WAY RUNNER

Roy "Wrong Way" Riegels
1929 Rose Bowl

It started with a fumble. It ended with a bigger fumble. It became the most famous wrong way run in football.

Georgia Tech was 30 yards from the University of California goal line. The ball was snapped. A Georgia player fumbled the ball. California's center Roy Riegels grabbed the loose ball. He spun around. The way to the end zone was clear.

Riegels ran like the wind. His feet flew over the turf. The goal line grew closer. The fans screamed. The players screamed. The coaches screamed. They all screamed the same thing. Riegels was running in the *wrong direction!*

Benny Lom, Riegels' teammate, took off in hot pursuit of the wrong way runner. The two men sprinted toward the goal. Riegels thought Lom was going to block for him. He was wrong again. Lom leaped just as Riegels reached the goal line. Riegels was tackled *six inches* from the wrong goal! "Wrong Way" Riegels didn't make a score—he made football history.

A SHORT BOMB

Eddie LeBaron, Dallas Cowboys, 1960

The Dallas Cowboys' new quarterback Eddie LeBaron poked his head out of the huddle. The ball was inches from the Washington Redskins' goal line.

Eddie studied the Redskins facing him from the line of scrimmage. What should he do; run or pass? The answer seemed obvious. A team only inches from the end zone would run.

The Redskins knew that. They expected the Cowboys' fullback to plunge through the center of the line. They braced for a run.

LeBaron took the snap. The Redskins surged forward. But Eddie did not hand off the ball to the fullback. He stepped back. He glanced sideways. Scurrying toward the goal was the Cowboys' tight end, Dick Bielski. Eddie fired a pass.

Bielski grabbed the ball and plunged over the goal line for a score! The unexpected pass was only *two inches long!* It was the shortest pass in NFL history.

16

ACE REPORTER

Colgate vs. Syracuse, 1897

They say newspaper reporters have ice water in their blood. J.V. King was a reporter with football in his. He proved it the day his old team, Colgate, played Syracuse.

King was on the sidelines. His derby hat sat neatly on his head. His pen and notebook were in his hands. He watched the game closely, making notes on each play. Suddenly a Syracuse player exploded from the line of scrimmage. The ball carrier had a clear shot for a touchdown run.

The crowd screamed. King did more than that. He decided not to let his old team down. He raced onto the field, right into the runner's path. The eager reporter threw his arms around the startled Syracuse runner. The two tumbled to the ground.

King fumbled his job as reporter because his tackle, not his writing, made the headlines.

FAKED FUMBLE

Oakland Raiders, 1978

Ten seconds remained on the clock. The Oakland Raiders trailed the San Diego Chargers, 20-14. Oakland had the ball. The chances of a score were slim.

Oakland lined up just 14 yards from the goal line. A pass into the end zone could tie the game. The extra point could win it.

Raiders' quarterback Ken Stabler hunched over the center. He took the snap and dropped back to pass. All of his receivers were covered. He held the ball, hoping to find someone. It was too late. A Charger charged into his side. If Stabler held onto the ball, the game would end. The only way to keep the game alive was a deliberate fumble.

Just before he fell, Stabler flipped the ball forward in a phony fumble. The ball was loose and alive!

Pete Banaszak, an Oakland halfback, chased the ball. If he picked it up, he would be tackled instantly. The game would be over.

Banaszak kicked the ball toward the goal line. Another Raider, tight end Dave Casper, tapped it into the end zone. He fell on the "fumble" for a TD! The game was tied. The point after was good. The Raiders won.

Dave Casper kicks a loose "fumble" into the end zone for a game-winning TD!

FEARLESS FOOTBALL

Georgia Tech vs. Cumberland, 1916

It started with an invitation to play football. It ended in a scoring disaster.

Cumberland College didn't have a great football team. The small college's president asked Georgia Tech for a game anyway. Georgia insisted that Cumberland send a check for $3,000. Georgia Tech would get the money if Cumberland did not place a team on the field. Cumberland agreed. After all, the game was Cumberland's idea.

But the First World War was underway. It looked like Cumberland would not have a team. Without a team, Cumberland would lose the $3,000. It was more than the school could spare.

Some Cumberland law students read the agreement. It said that Cumberland had to "place a team on the field." It didn't say the team had to know how to play football!

The "team" Cumberland sent wasn't a team at all. It was just a group of college men who hoped to save their school a whopping $3,000. The "team" didn't even practice.

It showed. By the end of the first half, Georgia Tech had 18 touchdowns! The final quarters were shortened to ten minutes each. The disaster didn't end until Georgia scored 222 points. Cumberland ended up with 0! It was the highest football score ever! But the valiant Cumberland "team" saved the $3,000!

WHIFFLE BALL

Mike Clark, Dallas Cowboys, 1969

Seventy thousand excited fans could not believe their eyes. The Dallas Cowboys were losing to the Cleveland Browns. The score was 38-7. Dallas was desperate.

To get the ball back, Dallas decided to try an onside kick. That's a short kick that can be recovered by the kicking team if the kick is done just right.

Both teams expected the short kick. Every player on the field was tense.

Mike Clark was the Cowboys' placekicker. He placed the ball on the rubber kicking tee. The tee would hold the ball at just the right angle. Mike's magic foot would do the rest.

Mike stepped off the distance he needed for a running kick. He turned. The ball was on its tee. Mike signaled he was ready. The Browns and Cowboys were ready. The fans held their breaths.

Mike ran toward the ball. He set his left foot firmly down and raised his right foot. He kicked.

Twenty-three players converged in the middle of the field. All eyes searched the sky for the ball. *It was gone!*

The ball hadn't moved! It was still on the tee where Mike put it. He missed it completely. The kick wasn't a kick. It was Mike Clark's most embarrassing fumbler.

Head-on Collision

Two star players decided to give a rival punt returner a tackling he would never forget. Their plan was to hit the unsuspecting player from both sides. They planned their collision for the moment the player's attention was on a high punt.

The kick went high into the air. The two tacklers raced downfield, one on each side. The punt returner had his eyes on the ball.

The tacklers turned toward their rival. They dug in their heels. They put down their heads. With legs churning, the tacklers flew across the gridiron. As the rival grabbed the ball, the tacklers dived toward him. Their flying tackles were timed to hit the ball carrier at the same instant.

The ball carrier jumped out of the way. The flying tacklers hit head-on. Both fell to the ground, *knocked-out cold!*

A PLAY TO BEAT THE BAND

California Golden Bears, 1982

Four seconds remained on the clock. A Stanford Cardinals' field goal put them ahead of the California Golden Bears by one point. The score was 20-19. The game was almost over. After all, what could happen in four seconds?

To guard against a California kickoff return, the Cardinals' kicker booted a feeble punt. The ball floated into Golden Bear Kevin Moen's hands. Kevin dashed downfield. He tossed the ball to a teammate a split second before being tackled. The teammate headed for the goal posts. Just before he was tackled, he lateraled the ball.

The clock ran out. The game was officially over. The stadium went wild. Stanford had won. Fans poured onto the gridiron. The Stanford band lined up in the end zone for a victory march.

But the play was still alive! Until the ball was dead, the game could continue.

The third Golden Bear runner still had the ball. Each step took him closer to the goal line. He flipped the ball to one more Bear just before he was hit. That Bear tossed the ball.

There was Kevin Moen! Kevin caught the ball

for a second time. He ran headlong into the band. He charged through the startled musicians, knocking them left and right. Suddenly he was over the goal line for a touchdown! California won the game— with a *little* help from Stanford's band!

Kevin Moen joins the Stanford band as he weaves his way to a winning score!

MUD HUDDLE

Bill Chipley,
Washington & Lee Generals, 1946

Why do firemen wear red suspenders?
To keep their pants up.
Why do football players wear different colored jerseys?

Well, they're supposed to help tell the teams apart. It doesn't always work.

The gridiron was a muddy mess as the Washington & Lee Generals trotted out to meet the West Virginia Mountaineers. Both teams wore bright, clean, uniforms. That didn't last long.

Soon everyone was coated with mud. The mud got thicker with each play. The teams flopped up and down the field like frogs in a pond. By the fourth quarter, the players looked like mud men.

The score was tied, 0-0. Suddenly, West Virginia was in scoring range a few yards from the Generals' goal! The ball was snapped.

Defending General Bill Chipley smashed into the play. He fell down, stunned by a solid rap on the helmet. He staggered back to a huddle.

The mud-caked team called their next play.

Chipley shook his head. He had never heard that play called before. He asked another player what he was supposed to do.

The Mountaineers became suspicious. They counted the players in their huddle. There were 12! They had an extra man.

Chipley had bumbled into the *wrong* huddle! Or should we say, **mud**dle?

WIND TUNNEL TOUCHDOWN

Clair Scott, Indiana Hoosiers, 1913

It was a kicker's nightmare. Clair Scott, the Indiana Hoosiers' punter, was deep in his own end zone. A stiff breeze blew into his face. His opponents, the Iowa Hawkeyes, were on the Hoosiers' 3-yard line. The best kick in the world would not be good enough. The worst kick? Well, that's what was coming.

Scott took the snap from center. He held the ball for a moment, then he kicked. His foot connected solidly with the ball. The pigskin rose high into the air, right into the howling wind.

The ball floated to the 20-yard line. It slowed to a stop, its momentum gone. Now the wind had it. The ball drifted backward! Like "Wrong Way" Riegels, it went the wrong direction. Soon it was over the goal line. Scott's fumbled punt sailed over 40 yards to get right back where it started.

Leo Dick, Iowa's punt returner, watched in amazement. He broke into a run. He raced into the Indiana end zone as the ball dropped from the sky. He grabbed it for an instant touchdown!

GIVEAWAY GAME

New York Giants, 1978

Victory was 28 seconds away for the New York Giants. One play would end the game to beat the Philadelphia Eagles, 17-12. All the Giants' quarterback, Joe Pisarcik, had to do was take the snap from center and fall on the ball. The clock would run out. New York would win.

Without explanation, a New York coach sent in a running play. The Giants could not believe it. It made no sense to risk losing the ball. The safest play would be for Pisarcik to fall to the ground with the ball.

The players argued in the huddle. Pisarcik shook his head. His job was to follow orders. That's what he would do.

The ball was snapped. Pisarcik took the ball. He handed it to teammate Larry Csonka. The handoff was *fumbled!* The ball bounced free.

Eagle defensive back Herman Edwards swooped over the ball. He grabbed it and ran into the end zone. Philadelphia turned the Giants' ill-fated fumble into a winning score! The Eagles won, 19-17.

Herman Edwards (46) prepares to scoop up Joe Pisarcik's (9) fumble to win for the Eagles.

SNAFU FROM CENTER

Jack Concannon, Chicago Bears, 1969

A center's job is to snap the ball when the quarterback calls the signal. It doesn't always work the way it's supposed to.

Jack Concannon was the Chicago Bears' quarterback. Mike Pyle was the center. The Bears were playing the St. Louis Cardinals.

Concannon told Pyle to snap the ball the instant Pyle heard his voice. The idea was to get the play moving before the Cardinals were ready.

The Bears lined up for the play. The Cardinals hunched down over the line of scrimmage. Concannon set himself behind Pyle, ready to call the snap. But something was wrong. *One of the Bears was not in the right place!*

Concannon stepped back. He shouted to the referee for a time out.

Pyle heard the shout. His orders were to "fire" the ball. He did. It shot back through his legs like a cannonball. It hit Concannon's knee and zoomed into the air.

Cardinal linebacker Larry Stallings couldn't believe his eyes. The ball dropped into his hands. Already running full speed, he kept going. The

Bears watched in surprise as the Cardinal raced all the way for a touchdown! The fumbled play cost the Bears the game.

Dirty Doughnuts

Football players are big men with big appetites. Some eat anything to stay big. Others simply eat *everything*.

Lyle Blackwood of the Baltimore Colts spotted a box of doughnuts in the training room. Nearby was a vat filled with hot wax used to treat muscle sprains. Players put injured arms or feet into the wax to ease the pain.

Blackwood dipped a few doughnuts into the wax. He stacked them on a plate. They looked like glazed doughnuts. A close look revealed that some were "decorated" with hair.

A teammate entered the room. His eyes lighted up when he saw the "frosted" doughnuts. He popped them down, wax, hair and all! *YECH!*

TRICK PLAY

New York Giants, 1933

When is the center not the center?
When he's on the end.

Mel Hein was the center for the New York Giants. His usual job was to pass the ball between his legs to quarterback Harry Newman. This time it was different.

Just before the play was called, the player on Hein's left stepped out of the line. That left Hein on the end, not the center. Newman moved in behind Hein in a T formation. He put his hands under Hein's legs. He called for the snap.

Hein handed the ball to Newman. Newman immediately handed it back to Hein. By the rules, it was a forward pass. Hein was an eligible receiver because he was on the *end of the line!*

Newman dropped back. He pretended to have the ball. The Bears couldn't see he didn't have it so they chased him. Newman "stumbled" and fell.

Meanwhile, Hein slipped the ball under his jersey. While the Bears chased Newman, Hein strolled downfield. A Bear saw Hein sneaking toward the goal. The trick play was discovered and Hein was tackled before he could score. It was a trick play that *almost* worked.

THE EMPTY BOWL

Washington State vs. San Jose State, 1955

Weather is always a factor in football. Tens of thousands of fans turn out to watch their favorite teams compete on bright fall football afternoons. In bad weather, not as many brave the elements.

But football fans are a hardy lot. It takes a lot to keep them away from the stadium.

On November 12, 1955, the weather finally won. Washington State and San Jose State teams tried to warm up, but the stadium was bitter cold. The temperature was zero! A harsh wind made it feel even colder.

Players flapped their arms. They blew on their fingers. They ran and jumped to keep warm. At last it was time for the opening kickoff. The teams took the field. The referee signaled for the clock to start. The kicker headed for the ball. He kicked. It was the moment the stadium usually trembles with the roar of the excited crowd. This time the stands were as silent as a grave.

Only *one* person had bought a ticket to the frosty affair!

EXCUSES, EXCUSES

Rafael Septien, Placekicker, Dallas Cowboys

Teacher: Where is your homework, Johnny?
Johnny: *My dog ate it.*

Nobody would be silly enough to use that excuse for missing homework. But silly excuses are easy for one well-known football player. He's Rafael Septien, the placekicker. Here are some of his best fumbled attempts to explain poor kicks.

Coach: That was a terrible kick. What happened?
Septien: *The grass was too long.* (The grass was artificial turf!)

Coach: You blew that kick, Rafael. What's your excuse this time?
Septien: *The clock distracted me.*

Coach: You call that a kick? What went wrong?
Septien: *My helmet was too tight.*

Coach: You missed that field goal! Why?
Septien: *The ball holder put the ball upside down!*

The next time you forget to do homework, say your dog ate it! You don't even have to own a dog.

Another great excuse! "Wet" turf trips up placekicker Rafael Septien.

HEADS, YOU—*OUCH*—LOSE

Leon Hart, Notre Dame, 1946

Leon Hart was eager for his first big game. Notre Dame's coach, Frank Leahy, called him off the bench. "Get in there, Leon," Leahy said to the excited young player. The 17 year old college freshman leaped to his feet

Leon means "lion." Anyone named "Lion" Hart is sure to be as bold as his namesake. Leon charged off the bench. He put his head down and raced across the field toward the Notre Dame huddle.

Bob Livingstone, the Irish halfback, ran from the opposite direction. The two players were on a collision course!

Leon smashed into Livingstone. The startled halfback fell to the turf. He was *knocked out cold*.

Leon struggled to his feet. The new kid had fumbled his first appearance by knocking out one of his own players.

Luckily, the "lion-hearted" young player did not let his embarrassing fumbler affect his career. He became an All-American and won the Heisman Trophy as well!

THE PERRY FERRY

William "The Refrigerator" Perry, Chicago Bears, 1985

William "The Refrigerator" Perry was everybody's favorite. The "Fridge" was too big to play basketball, but that didn't stop the 325 pound giant from carrying a teammate like a basket!

Perry's team, the Chicago Bears, was mashing the Dallas Cowboys, 44-0. Perry's usual position was defensive tackle, but sometimes he played fullback. He could blast a hole through a line wide enough for a freight train.

The Bears were 2 yards from another touchdown. Perry went in to open a path for the team's running back, Walter Payton. Payton was a little guy, in refrigerator sizes. He weighed *only* 202 pounds.

Payton took the handoff and headed for the hole Perry made. But the Cowboys had plugged the hole. The "Fridge" sized up the situation in a second. If Payton couldn't run with the ball, Perry would run with it— and Payton!

The huge Bear picked up his teammate like a

basket. With the 200-pounder safely in his grip, the "Fridge" rumbled toward the goal line. He was stopped before he could score. The play was illegal. Perry grinned. He was only trying to help his teammate, he said.

Look Before You Leap

Bob Fenimore of the Oklahoma A&M Aggies was certain he was going to score a touchdown. He raced full speed toward the goal line. All he had to do was reach it before a tackler got him.

After an outstanding 45-yard run, the goal line appeared at last. Fenimore leaped into the air in a desperate dive for the end zone. He sailed over the line and skidded to a stop.

The trouble was the line *wasn't* the goal line. It was the *10-yard line!* The dramatic dive ended Fenimore's chance for glory.

SIDELINE SECRET

Tommy Lewis,
Alabama Crimson Tide, 1954

Alabama's Crimson Tide was one point behind the Owls of Rice, 7-6. But the winner of the important Cotton Bowl game was still undecided.

Suddenly Alabama's quarterback fumbled. The Owls recovered. The Owls had a chance to score!

The ball was snapped. Owls' halfback Dick Moegle tucked the pigskin against his side and started to run. The path was clear for a touchdown. *Almost!*

Tommy Lewis, Alabama's captain, sat on the bench as the lonesome Owl flew by on his way to the goal line. He leaped to his feet and took off after Moegle.

Lewis ran seven yards like a man on fire. Helmetless, he smashed into Moegle. The surprise tackle knocked Moegle to the ground. His touchdown run was ended by Tommy's illegal sideline tackle but officials awarded the Owls a score. The fumbler cost one touchdown. The Owls ended up winning the game!

Tommy Lewis (42) leaps off the bench and onto the field to tackle unsuspecting Dick Moegle. Moegle earned a TD without crossing the goal line!

PLEASE PASS THE HELMET!

George Woodruff,
Georgia Bulldogs, 1910

The fog was thick enough to slice. Unfortunately, fans could still see the scoreboard. The Georgia Bulldogs were being eaten alive by the Sewanee Tigers, 15-6.

Georgia's "Kid" Woodruff stared into the dense fog. He knew the direction of the end zone, but the goal posts were hidden. A brilliant idea crossed his mind. The Tigers were having as much trouble seeing as he was!

Woodruff huddled with his team. The Bulldogs lined up at scrimmage. Woodruff called the play. The ball was snapped.

With a sly smile on his lips, Woodruff slipped the ball out of sight under his arm. He pulled off his leather helmet with his free hand. The Tigers rumbled toward him.

Woodruff raised his passing arm. He cranked it back and threw a long toss. His *helmet* sailed through the fog high over the Tigers' heads. The Tigers turned away to follow the "ball."

Certain that nobody was on to his trick,

Woodruff passed the real ball to receiver Bob McWhorter. As the Tigers chased the tossed helmet, McWhorter scrambled for a touchdown!

TURK'S TWIST

Turk Edwards,
Washington Redskins, 1940

Football is a rough game. Injuries happen when players crash together. The safest part of a game is the coin toss, right? *Wrong!*

The Redskins and Giants were set to clash. The opposing captains walked to midfield for the coin toss. The ref was ready with a shiny silver dollar in his hand.

Turk Edwards was the Redskins' captain. He was big and rough and ready for action. His opponent, Giants' captain Mel Hein, was an old friend. But today they would battle for football glory.

The ref flipped the coin. It spun to the ground as Hein called, "Heads!" The coin landed tails. The Redskins would receive. The Giants would kick off.

The captains shook hands. Hein turned toward his sideline. Turk Edwards spun toward his.

The Redskins' captain dropped to the ground with a shout of pain. Turk's cleats had dug into

the soft turf. When he turned, his foot did not
turn with him. His leg twisted. His knee was badly
injured!

Turk Edwards was carried from the field. He
was embarrassed. He knew he would be out of the
game. But the future Hall of Famer did not know
his stumble *ended his career forever!*

THE 200 YARD TOUCHDOWN

Ray Dowd, Lehigh University, 1918

Everyone knows a football field is 100 yards long. One player had to run over 200 yards to score. How did he manage a fumbler like that?

Ray Dowd of Lehigh University was the player. In an exciting play near his opponent's end zone, Ray got turned around. He had the ball. He knew his job was to run. So, that's what he did.

Ray raced down the entire field. He burst into the end zone. Nobody stopped him because he ran the whole distance the *wrong way!*

Suddenly Ray realized his fumbler. He knew he was at the wrong end.

Ray was a gutsy player. He put his blunder behind him. He spun around and ran the opposite way. He roared over the turf for the *second time in the same play!* This time he made it into the correct end zone for a touchdown. His breathless run of 210 yards was a record.

TEAMMATE TACKLE

Bobby Yandell,
Mississippi Rebels, 1941

When is a perfect tackle perfectly *awful*? When a player tackles the wrong man. When is a perfectly awful tackle worse? When the wrong man tackled is on *your* team!

The score was 0-0. The Ole Miss Rebels and the Mississippi State Bulldogs were playing for the Southeastern Conference Championship. The Rebels had the ball. On the snap from center, Rebel tailback Junior Hovious tossed a pass downfield.

The ball soared neatly into the waiting hands of Ray Poole, a Rebel end. Poole broke away from an Ole Miss player who was determined to tackle him.

Poole headed for the goal line. The field was wide open. The only player close to him was his own teammate, Bobby Yandell. Poole knew Yandell would block for him if he needed help. Poole raced for the touchdown.

But Yandell was confused. Seeing a player running with the ball, the only thing he could think of was "*tackle!*" And that's what he did.

Yandell plunged into his teammate, dropping him in midfield. There was no touchdown. To make matters worse, the terrible tackle cost the Rebels the game—and the title, too!

Mississippi Rebel Bobby Yandell's fumbled tackle downed his own teammate and lost the championship, too.

GATORADE FIRST AID

Iona College, 1987

It's a football tradition. At the end of a victorious game the winning players douse their coach with Gatorade. It's a symbol of a sweet victory. But sometimes Gatorade gaiety gets sticky.

Iona College in New York was in the football basement. They had lost 27 straight games. To everyone's surprise they came up a winner in a contest against St. Peter's. They buried their opponent, 27-0.

What a great idea to drench the coach, the players thought. It could be years before Iona would win another game.

The winning players surrounded their coach. Up went the bucket. Down came the Gatorade. The coach was soaked. Players and fans screamed.

One player helping to drown the coach jumped into the air with joy. It was a terrible fumbler.

The player came down like a rock. He landed in a heap. He twisted his knee so badly he couldn't play for weeks. Oh, the agony of victory!

FAMOUS FOOTBALL TRICKS

Carlisle Indians, 1903

Football fans know the game is played according to strict rules. That's why there are "zebra shirts" on the field. Officials keep the game honest.

In the early years, football rules weren't so strict. Tricks were easy. The Carlisle Indians were experts.

Once the Indians wore jerseys with football-shaped patches sewn on. When the ball was snapped from center, the real ball was lost among the patches. Confused opponents chased everyone hoping one had the real thing.

The trick backfired. Harvard heard about the "patches" trick. The next week the Harvard coach painted all the game footballs bright red to match the color of Harvard's jerseys. Red footballs against Harvard's red shirts would be as confusing as Carlisle's patches. The teams agreed to play fair. The patches came off and brown balls were used to play.

But Carlisle had one more trick up its jersey. Late in the game, the Indians' quarterback hid the ball under a teammate's jersey. When the play started, all the Indians took off their leather helmets. They tucked them under their arms like footballs and ran toward the goal. The player with the hidden ball ran for a touchdown while Harvard chased the fakes. Pop Warner, the Indians' coach—he's the man Pop Warner football is named for—roared with laughter. That is, he laughed until Harvard won, 12-11!

PLAYER PYRAMID

Cornell vs. Princeton, 1965

The Cornell Big Red knew the Princeton Tigers would try a field goal. They also knew the Tigers' kicker, Charlie Gogolak, was good. But the Big Red had a plan.

The minute the Tigers came out of their huddle, Cornell was ready. Two Cornell giants, both six feet, five inches tall, planted their feet firmly on the turf. Two more Cornell defenders scrambled onto the tall players' shoulders seconds before the ball was snapped. The four men formed a wall over *twelve feet high!*

Gogolak was stumped. Then he saw that the Big Red wall was lined up *crooked.* Gogolak carefully aimed his kicking foot. He hoped to send the ball to one side of the wall, not over it. The kick went wide. Gogolak missed the field goal!

The Tigers got their revenge later when Gogolak scored two field goals. Both went straight over the Big Red human wall. Cornell fumbled because their wall defense crumbled.

THE YAWN OF
THE CENTURY

Notre Dame vs. Army, 1946

West Points' famed Cadets and the Fighting Irish of Notre Dame were longtime rivals. Their annual contests were football at its best. Fans waited months to watch the powerful teams collide.

Notre Dame went into a slump. It lost two games in two years to Army. The scores were embarrassing for Notre Dame. One year Army won, 59-0. The following year Army won, 48-0.

Notre Dame was much stronger the next year. Army and Notre Dame were ranked tops in the country in 1946. The annual game would be "The Game of the Century." Tickets cost as much as $200. Fans expected great football. They knew scoring would be high. It would be a match of giants they could talk about for years.

For 60 minutes the teams crashed into one another on the gridiron. The ball went back and forth. But it *never* crossed the goal line for a score!

The highly advertised "Game of the Century" ended up a *scoreless tie!*

High-scoring hopes turned to ho-hum in the game nobody won. Army and Notre Dame leave the field after a (yawn) scoreless tie.

TEAM TURNABOUT

St. Louis Cardinals, 1966

The game was a heart-stopper. The St. Louis Cardinals and Dallas Cowboys were locked in a 10-10 tie. Less than two minutes remained in the game. Dallas was forced to kick.

Dallas kicker Danny Villanueva prepared to punt. The St. Louis Cardinals prepared to return Danny's kick. Nobody expected what really happened.

The ball was snapped to Danny. He glanced up. To his surprise the Cardinal defense was running away. Rather than block Danny's kick, they ran downfield. They planned to block for their teammate who would return the punt. They forgot Danny. Danny was all alone.

Danny grabbed the ball. He was a kicker, not a runner. But with nobody to stop him, he ran. None of the Cardinals saw him. They were running the other way!

Danny scurried downfield unnoticed. He was finally tackled, but not before turning the Cardinals' fumbled punt return into a *23-yard gain!*

THE WATER POLO PLAY

Oklahoma Sooners vs. Oklahoma Aggies, 1904

Water polo is not what the Oklahoma Sooners and Oklahoma A & M Aggies had in mind.

The wind was blowing hard. The gridiron was perilously close to Cottonwood Creek. A high kick sent the ball skyward. The wind grabbed it. There was nothing the players could do but watch as the ball drifted toward the river. It landed in the icy water with a splash and floated downstream like a duck.

The rules said that whoever recovered the ball got possession. That meant either team could fish the ball out of the bubbling creek.

As an Aggie player poked at the bobbing ball with a stick, a Sooner player toppled him into the creek. The two fought over the ball that slipped from their grips like a wet fish. Other players joined the melee. Soon the river was full of football players.

At last a Sooner back who could do the backstroke recovered the slippery ball. He paddled downstream until he was past the Aggie goal line.

He clambered from the creek and carried the ball
onto the field for a touchdown!

THE KICK-ME CALL

Abner Haynes, Dallas Texans, 1962

In a sudden-death overtime, the game ends when the first score is made. The choice to receive or to kick can decide the game. The best choice is to receive. That gives the receiving team the first chance to score. Sometimes things go wrong.

The Dallas Texans and the Houston Oilers had played to a thrilling 17-17 tie. But it was the AFL championship game. It had to continue until there was a winner.

If the Texans won the coin toss, they would have two choices. They could kick or choose a goal to defend. A strong wind was blowing. The Texans' coach decided to receive. He wanted the wind at his team's back. It would make kicking a field goal easier. He told captain Abner Haynes to choose to defend the goal facing the clock.

The Texans won the toss. The referee turned to Haynes. Without thinking, Haynes said, "We'll kick to the clock." He meant he wanted to *defend* the goal facing the clock, but he said *kick*. That meant the Oilers could choose the best field position.

The terrible blunder gave the advantage to the Oilers. With the wind at their backs, the Oilers kicked the winning field goal. Abner Haynes' fumbled decision cost the Texans the *title!*

Abner Haynes fumbled coin-toss call led to a win for his opponents and a loss for his own team. Better wear a helmet next time, Abner.

Tender Tacklers

The punt returner had injured his ankle. It was painful, but he insisted on staying in the game.

The opposing team punted. The injured player hobbled downfield as the ball sailed over his head. In the meantime, the kicking team raced toward him.

The injured player reached the ball a second before his tacklers arrived. Unable to run, he braced himself for the tackle.

It never came. One of the tacklers took pity on the hobbling ball carrier. "Don't hit him!" he shouted to his teammates.

The tacklers put their hands on the surprised punt returner. They gently lifted him into the air and then lowered him softly to the ground. It was the friendliest tackle ever made!

LOOP THE LOOP

Sam McAllester,
Tennessee Volunteers, 1904

Today's hi-tech football equipment can't match the "space technology" Tennessee fullback Sam McAllester dreamed up in 1904.

McAllester's equipment included a tough leather belt with two strong loops attached. Nobody knew exactly what the the loops were for—until it was too late.

At the snap, the ball was handed to McAllester. He tucked the ball next to his body. He leaped forward. Two Tennessee backs ran to his side. McAllester climbed onto the back of one of his guards as if the crouching player were a step. At that moment the two backs grabbed the leather loops. With a powerful heave, the burly backfielders tossed McAllester over the line of scrimmage. For a second he was in space. When he came down, Tennessee had gained 5 yards!

The wacky "space shot" worked every time. It was so successful that the only touchdown scored was when McAllester was launched over the line into the end zone.

LAUGHTER DISASTER

Garo Yepremian,
Miami Dolphins, 1973

Garo Yepremian was from Cyprus where soccer was the favorite game. He didn't grow up with football, but he was an expert kicker. He left how to play football to others on his team.

Super Bowl VII raced to a lopsided finish. Garo's team, the Miami Dolphins, led the Washington Redskins, 14-0. Two minutes remained in the game.

The Dolphins decided to try a field goal. It was not needed to win, but extra points could prevent a disaster in case things went wrong.

The ball was snapped. Yepremian kicked as Redskin Bill Brundige blew through the line. He blocked the kick. The ball fell to the ground. It bobbled around like a playful puppy.

Garo stared at the loose ball. Most players would fall on the ball. The compact kicker from Cyprus picked it up and cocked his arm to *pass!*

The ball skittered off the tips of his fingers. It flipped into the air. Redskin Mike Bass grabbed the ball before it hit the ground. It was a pass interception! Bass ran 49 yards for a touchdown!

Luckily, the Dolphins won, but Yepremian's awful fumbler almost cost his team a perfect season.

Garo Yepremian (1) tries to turn a blocked kick into a forward pass. His famous Super Bowl fumbler made history instead.

HEIDI, HEIDI, HO HO!

Oakland Raiders vs.
New York Jets, 1968

Heidi is a favorite children's story. Football is a favorite sports fan's pastime. Television is the perfect place to watch both. But *not* at the same time!

Joe Namath was the Jets' star quarterback. Daryle Lamonica was the Raiders' quarterback. The two men led their teams in a great game of Sunday afternoon football. The score was close all the way. First one team went ahead, then the other took the lead. Finally, with only a minute left to play, the Jets led, 32-29. All they had to do to win was to hold on for 60 seconds.

Nobody expected the game to be so thrilling. Fans across the country were glued to their television sets.

Suddenly *Heidi* came on the air! The television network decided to show the children's classic because the game was lasting longer than usual. For millions of fans watching on television, the game was over. They missed the most exciting minute of the entire game!

With only 43 seconds left, Daryle Lamonica tossed a 43-yard touchdown pass! The Raiders jumped ahead. Only seconds remained. The Jets fumbled the kick after touchdown. Oakland recovered and scored again!

The game was over. The Raiders won while millions of upset football fans watched *Heidi!*

Daryle Lamonica didn't know it, but his 43-yard, winning TD pass was missed by millions who watched *Heidi* instead.

THE TERRIFIED TIGER

Peter Gowan,
Memphis State Tigers, 1971

Small but fast "Skeeter" Gowan of the Memphis State Tigers wanted to end his college football career in one piece. The best way was to *run and hide.*

Skeeter's final game was almost over. Memphis State was safely ahead of the San Jose Spartans. Gowan raced for the end zone with the ball. He made it past two Spartan defenders. The way was clear for a touchdown. But a big, snorting tackler was still hot on Skeeter's tail!

Skeeter zipped across the goal line. He was safe. He heard a voice. The Spartan tackler was still coming!

Skeeter dashed out of the end zone. The tackler didn't stop. Skeeter ran off the field. The tackler followed him.

Skeeter scooted up the bleachers as if they were giant stairs. He turned around. The grunting tackler had stopped at last . Skeeter was safe, but he stayed in the stand for ten more minutes. Better to be safe than sorry!

WRONG WAY, AGAIN

Jim Marshall, Minnesota Vikings, 1964

Pass, fumble, *fumbler!*
San Francisco 49er Billy Kilmer snagged the pass. He ran, but a flood of Viking tacklers mashed him to the ground. Kilmer fumbled.

Jim Marshall, a huge Viking lineman, had just charged through the 49ers' line. He spun around. He spotted the loose ball. He leaped over a 49er and grabbed it. He closed his arms around the ball and bounded for the goal line, 60 yards away.

The massive lineman bolted down the field. The fans were yelling. So were his teammates. Marshall was sure they were cheering him on. But they weren't cheering. They were trying to tell him he was running the *wrong way!*

It was too late! Marshall burst over the goal line for an automatic two points *for the other side!*

Luckily, the Vikings won the game in spite of Marshall's spectacular "Wrong Way Riegels" fumbler.

Jim Marshall (70) races for the end zone. Opponent Bruce Bosley (77) tells him his wrong-way run just cost Marshall's Vikings two points.

Pitiful Pass

Kickers are usually smaller than other football players. When Oiler kicker Tony Zendejas picked up a fumbled snap from center, he panicked. Rushing him like a herd of rhinos was the whole Miami Dolphin defense!

Tony did not want to be trampled. Rather than be caught with the ball, he tossed it into the air. The pitiful pass was snagged by a Dolphin. But unlucky Tony got munched anyway.

THE 12 MAN TEAM

Kansas Jayhawks vs.
Penn State Nittany Lions, 1969

The Orange Bowl raced to a dramatic finish. The Kansas Jayhawks held a 7 point lead over the Penn State Nittany Lions, 14-7. A little over a minute remained in the game. If Kansas could hold the lead, they would win.

A 47 yard Penn State pass changed everything. Suddenly the Lions were at Kansas' 3 yard line. Kansas had to hold the line or lose. To stop the Lions, the Kansas coach replaced his regular linebackers with two big tackles.

Kansas linebacker Rick Abernathy forgot to leave the field when his replacement came. Twelve Kansas players were on the field. Nobody noticed the extra man.

Each time the Lions tried to score, the Kansas 12 stopped them. With 15 seconds remaining, the Lions ran around the Jayhawks for a touchdown. Now the Lions were only one point behind.

An extra point kick would end the game in a tie. The Lions decided to run a 2 point play. If they failed, they would lose. The ball was snapped. The

12 man Kansas team stopped the play. The game ended in Kansas' favor, 14-13.

But there was a flag on the field! Someone had spotted Abernathy. Kansas was penalized.

The last play was run over. This time the Lions scored! The game ended again. The Lions won on the incredible Kansas 12 man football fumbler!

One of the worst fumblers in Orange Bowl history leads to this 2-point conversion by Penn State's Bob Campbell (23).

YIKES! NO SPIKES!

Dave Smith, Pittsburgh Steelers, 1971

A spike is when a runner slams the ball to the turf after scoring a touchdown. It's a sign of triumph. But you have to do it *after you cross the goal line!*

Dave Smith of the Pittsburgh Steelers raced downfield to catch a pass from Terry Bradshaw. Bradshaw fired. The ball soared toward Smith. Smith snatched it. He tucked it under his arm and dashed for the end zone.

Smith zigged. He zagged. Each step carried him closer to a TD. He sensed victory. He still had five yards to go when he raised the ball over his head for his touchdown spike.

The ball slipped. It bobbled. Smith *dropped* it! The ball fell to the ground and rolled out of the end zone. The fumbled spike cost the Steelers the ball. It also cost Smith his pride.

WAY BACK QUARTERBACK

Dallas Cowboys vs.
Miami Dolphins, 1972

Miami Dolphins' quarterback Bob Griese knew the idea in football is to move the ball forward.

It was Super Bowl VI. Miami trailed the Dallas Cowboys. Griese planted himself behind his center. He looked up just before the ball was snapped. On the other side of the line of scrimmage, Bob Lilly of the Dallas Cowboys stared back.

The Cowboys' huge defensive back braced himself for the chase. Once the ball was snapped, Lilly would explode. His target was Griese!

Griese took the snap. With the ball tightly in his grip, he stepped back. Lilly plunged forward. Griese stepped back again. Lilly kept coming. Griese started to run. Lilly ran faster. Griese faded back, back, back until it was too late!

Lilly plowed into Griese. The Dolphin quarterback toppled to the ground. Lilly had sacked him *29 yards behind the line of scrimmage!*

It was the *biggest* loss on a *single* play in Super Bowl history!

Bob Griese (12) runs for his life from charging tackler Bob Lilly (74) who sacks him 29 yards behind the line of scrimmage!

LOOSE PANTS DANCE

Y. A. Tittle,
Louisiana State Tigers, 1947

They should have issued Y. A. Tittle suspenders when they handed out uniforms.

Tittle was playing for the Louisiana State Tigers against the Mississippi Rebels. When a Mississippi pass landed in his hands, he knew exactly what to do. He started running for the end zone.

Unfortunately, a Mississippi player grabbed Y. A.'s belt. As Y. A. pulled away, so did the belt. His pants began to drop.

Y. A. held the ball with one hand and grabbed his pants with the other. As he ran toward the goal line, his pants slid lower with each step.

Almost certain of a touchdown, Y. A. switched hands to ward off a tackler. He held onto the ball, but he fumbled his pants! The pants fell down in front of 50,000 wildly laughing fans. Y. A. fell to the ground, robbed of a certain touchdown by his own pants!